FELICITY FINDS FASHION

A Gecko's Adventure in New York City

By Linda S. Gunther

Illustrated by Diana Wright Troxell

Carina turned the corner, holding her mum's hand, ready to begin a journey across the Atlantic Ocean. It was summer and Mum was taking Carina on a trip to visit Mum's sister, who lived in New York City.

The cruise ship terminal was bustling with vacationers anxious to get on the ship.

"Carina, you forgot to zip up your backpack. Oh, come on, luv, we can't stop. We're blocking the way," Mum said.

Carina didn't like being in such a large crowd. She preferred reading a book in her room with Felicity, her pet gecko.

"Ouch," eight-inch-long Felicity yelled out, bumping her head on the metal ramp after she fell out of Carina's backpack. Reaching for her hat, she scooted out of the way, running up onto the ship's deck as fast as a small gecko could go.

But where was Carina? Felicity's eyes darted everywhere, but no Carina! Her four short legs carried her from deck to deck, from the ship's central atrium area

to its expansive theater,

and then up to the deck 12 "Welcome Aboard" buffet.

to the grand dining room,

BUT NO CARINA!

For the next few days, Felicity searched everywhere on the giant cruise ship for Carina, sleeping in storage areas and finding ants to eat near the outdoor barbeque.

On day 2, she was spotted by a ship worker who tried to catch her with a giant black net.

On day 3, there was the curious passenger who followed her down the jogging path, reaching out to grab her at every turn.

On day 4, she hid in a pile of laundry.

On day 5, Felicity went down to the swimming pool and took a dip. The pool water felt refreshing, as it cooled Felicity's dry skin.

Wow, look at that beautiful woman, the only passenger sitting out by the pool in the early morning sun. She's reading a fashion magazine. I LOVE fashion, Felicity thought.

Felicity tiptoed over to the lounge chair where the glamorous woman sat. She perched herself on the umbrella for a good view of the glossy photographs in the magazine. With one eye on the fashions and the other eye looking out for Carina, Felicity spent an enjoyable morning.

Spotting a glass of water, Felicity jumped down onto the table and stretched out her long slithery tongue for a quick slurp. Noticing a few ants crawling around, she snatched some up. "Yum, ants are scrumptious."

Just then, the beautiful woman stood up and began scooping up her sunglasses, lotion, towel, and water bottle. Then, oh no, Felicity tumbled down into the woman's designer bag.

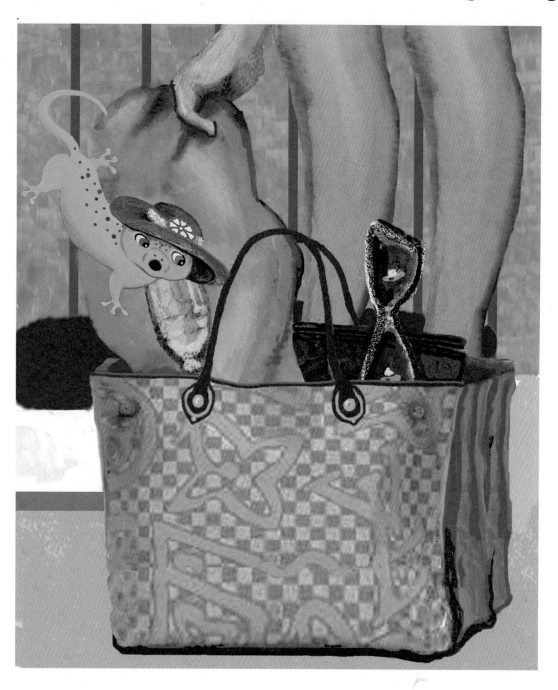

I'll never find Carina now, Felicity thought.

A few minutes later, she came flying out of the leather handbag, falling onto a fluffy towel, and then was pressed down into what seemed like a suitcase. Peeking out, she looked around and noticed a luggage tag that read, "Simone Parker." Then, she eyed a porthole, and through it she could see a magnificent statue.

Felicity tried to wriggle out of the suitcase, when suddenly Simone closed it, zipped it up, and sang out, "New York City, here I come!"

New York City? Is that where we're going? Felicity felt scared. Finding Carina would be even more impossible now, she worried.

Suddenly tired, she fell asleep, dreaming of her life at home in England with Carina.

When Felicity opened her eyes, she could see many pretty women rushing about. Some were laughing, some fixing their hair, and some looking into large mirrors.   Several were putting on clothes — skirts, blouses, and dresses of various styles and colors.

"Fashion Week is divine. We are lucky models," one woman said, giggling, as she twirled around, her dress swishing out like a fan. Felicity suddenly felt her tail being tugged from behind.

"A mouse. Help, it's a mouse," a woman screamed and jumped up onto a chair.

The mouse scurried into a hole in the wall. Felicity followed the mouse, as she was afraid the woman would spot her and then maybe scream even louder.

The mouse stared at Felicity. "And you? Where do you think you are going? Why do you follow me? Pourquoi ('Why')?"

Felicity hesitated and then said, "Um, I-I didn't want to be discovered, so I ran in here behind you."

"A gecko with a hat? Oooh la la," the mouse squeaked.

Felicity's body slumped, as she replied, "I wear a hat so people will know I'm a girl."

Laughing, the mouse said, "Oui, that makes sense."

Felicity peeked back through the hole. One of the models was wearing the most gorgeous flowing dress Felicity had ever seen.

"Ooh," Felicity exclaimed, "SO ELEGANT!"

From behind the red velvet curtain, Felicity and Lisette watched as model after model, walked down the fashion runway, showing off their chic clothes to the audience.

"Oh my!" Felicity gasped.

"Mon Cherie, do you wish to wear clothes just like those?" the mouse asked.

"What do you mean? I'm just a gecko with two different colored eyes. I'm not pretty enough to wear such clothes."

"Nonsense, you look fine," insisted Lisette. "I am the best seamstress in all of Europe. Straighten up, Miss Felicity. The runway awaits you."

"I wish I could wear such lovely things," Felicity remarked, sighing.

"Oui, very pretty, a French gown from Paris," said the mouse.

"How do you know that?" Felicity asked.

"Because I am Lisette, haute couture mouse from Paris, France. Come with me, Cherie," she replied.

Perched on Simone's hat, Felicity wore a summer beach outfit and carried a beach ball down the runway.

Next, Felicity went down the runway with another model, both of them in daytime outfits, smart business suits - perfect for a day at the office.

Then, Lisette dressed Felicity for winter. Felicity was in heaven, sitting atop the gorgeous model's ski hat.

Finally, Lisette dressed Felicity in an elegant midnight blue evening gown, Felicity's favorite color, with lots of sparkling rhinestone accents.

A dream had come true for Felicity. Yes, she was an ordinary gecko from a small English village, and her eyes didn't match. Yet, she was wearing the most gorgeous clothes and modeling at a New York fashion show.

As the fashion show ended, Felicity started to feel sad, thinking how much she missed Carina. Exhausted, she crawled into Simone's leather bag, and quickly fell asleep.

Suddenly the bag was lifted. As Simone shouted out her goodbye to the other models, Felicity waved to Lisette, who blew her a kiss.

Simone flew down the street. "Taxi! Taxi," she yelled. And, once again, Felicity tumbled out of the bag. Picking herself up, she raced into the park, away from the crowds of people on the street. She kept going through a large iron gate and into a world of animal sounds.

She felt thirsty. When Felicity spotted a puddle, she ran over as fast as she could.

"Yes Mum, I like the gorilla. He's funny. But I can't really enjoy this holiday after losing my gecko."

Felicity was startled by the English accent coming from the little girl.

Something moved by Carina's feet. "Felicity! Mum, look! Look, my gecko!"

Just then, the wind came up and a page from a newspaper went flying by them. Carina scooped up Felicity to give her a hug as her mum picked up the paper.

"Carina, I don't believe this," her mum exclaimed.

When Carina looked over at the newspaper, she saw the photograph of a beautiful model with something unusual sitting on her hat. The headline read, "FASHION WEEK: GECKO STEALS THE SHOW!

Felicity's eyes sparkled.

The End

Acknowledgements

Felicity Finds Fashion is a tribute to the fashion world in New York City as well as the joy of life in merry old England. I have lived in both places and they will always be in my heart.

Thanks to Laurel Ornitz for her helpful editing.

And a very special thank you to Diana Wright Troxell, my gifted and inventive illustrator. You are amazing.

My granddaughter, Taylor, inspired Felicity's character. She loves fashion just like Felicity. I love you Tay.

81304634R00015

Made in the USA
Lexington, KY
14 February 2018